PRAISE

"Felicity invites young readers into a whimsical rhyming world of our magical holiday characters. Laugh along in her lighthearted exploration of Gommet as she shows us just 'Where the Holidays Go!'"

Ronne Sisco
Director of Education
Endicott First Presbyterian Nursery School
Endicott, NY

"While teaching kindergarten, I had the privilege of hosting Felicity Fox as a guest author in my classroom at George F. Johnson Elementary School. After learning about the writing process, the children had the opportunity to learn from Felicity as she shared her book, Where the Holidays Go. In this imaginative story my students traveled to the holiday city of Gommet to experience familiar traditions in a unique and amusing way. By meeting a "real" author, in person, at the age of 5, I would hope to inspire these students to one day become authors themselves."

Lynn Gilyard
Retired Kindergarten Teacher
George F. Johnson Elementary School
Endicott, NY

"Felicity Fox's heart-warming story takes the reader on a unique journey to Gommet where the holiday traditions are delightful! What a magical story for both children and grown-ups alike!"

Sonja Lowe
First Grade Teacher
George F. Johnson Elementary School
Endicott, NY

"Where the Holidays Go is a delightful and whimsical story that will have children wanting to read it over and over!"

Josephine Ciotoli
Third Grade Teacher
George F. Johnson Elementary School
Endicott, NY

"Felicity Fox has captured the imagination of every child's dreams. What child doesn't like the holidays?"

Mary Jo Law
Retired Children's Librarian
Hancock Central School
Hancock, NY

WHERE THE HOLIDAYS GO

… The Holiday City where Santa trick-or-treats,
Pumpkins have feet, and Holiday Characters meet …

Written by
Felicity Fox

Illustrated by
Dan Buckley

ISBN Hardback: 978-1-64085-618-9
ISBN Paperback: 978-1-64085-617-2

WHERE THE HOLIDAYS GO is the first in this series.
Coming Soon:

Gommet's Beginnings: Where the Holidays Started

Gommet's Expansions: Where the Holidays Went

Gommet's Confusion: Where the Holidays Mixed-Up

DEDICATION

I dedicate this book to my beautiful babies, my son Harrison and my daughter Harley. I love you beyond words, and beyond all the hugs and kisses in the world! You make me proud every single day. You are both beautiful, worthy, capable, and smart. You can do anything! **Numbers 6: 24-26**.

When I originally wrote Where the Holidays Go, I researched the best method to get my book from idea to tangible form. I found an editor and together, we made this book the completed copy you are seeing. When my brother agreed to illustrate my book, I was floored with gratitude and excitement. His talent is second to none and if I'm being honest, my work would be lifeless without his absolutely amazing work. I can never thank him enough.

When the book was in the final format, I knew the task ahead to get it published. My fear wasn't a lack of interest, but a fear I would lose my creative vision in handing my book over. I wanted to know my book would be as I wanted it to be but I couldn't guarantee this if I went a traditional publishing route. I decided to self-publish and I was blessed by my choice. Within months, the wonderful Talia Moore of D.T. Productions turned this book into a musical! The lovely ladies at the Endicott Visitor's Center sold this book and asked me to create a carousel book. (If you're not local to Endicott, NY, see my website www.thefelicityfoxhouse.com for information on these things). I was grateful and excited and forged ahead. Years later, I still receive invitations to do author visits and felt the push to do more with this book. I wanted to edit some paragraphs out, to make it available in several forms, to update the front and back covers, and to make an overall noticeable change that would make the book more attractive to the eye. I am richly blessed to be published by Author Academy Elite. Through this, I am able to present to you this second edition!

Thanks to every single person who has supported me through the years. I specifically thank my amazing family and incredible friends. As a child, God put this dream in my heart, and I knew I was meant to make it happen.

With this book, I wish two things for you. 1) To find a timeless story that will enchant your hearts and souls, 2) a tangible experience to bring this magic to life! When this series is complete (three more books to come!), like the musical based on this book, there will be live and in person experiences available. Please check my website for the most up-to-date information in regards to all things Gommet, including the experiences, author visits, book signings, and the other three books in this holiday series! These are all on their way!!

Thank you to my friends for their beautiful endorsements. Thank you for all the support. As always, my prayer is that God is illuminated through each and every thing I do. **Colossians 3:23**

Love, Felicity

Do you wonder where the holidays go?

In what big red barn is Santa's sleigh stowed?

What happens to scarecrows past Halloween?

Cupid and leprechauns? Know what I mean?

A secret city for holidays exists.

With magical nooks and magnificent twists.

This enchanting place, named Gommet, is miles wide;

it's a world where holiday characters reside.

This city is where the holidays meet,

pilgrims cook and Santa Claus trick or treats.

Six holidays diligently work their due,

creating goodies and granting wishes, too.

Thousands of apple seeds are planted each day,

meticulously placed in the sun's warm rays.

Crisp apples are crushed into cider each noon,

pumpkins plump up, later peonies in June.

On Valentine Avenue the fairies are quick

to bake, frost, and decorate, lickety-split.

They'll help Cupid to deliver all special things,

though he is quickest with his turbo-charged wings.

The houses here are heart-shaped and shiny,

red, white, and pink, satin-soft, teeny-tiny.

Lampposts and mailboxes are draped with streamers,

filled with roses and bright wishes from dreamers.

Only a few stoves brew love through each day,

it takes just a little to go a long way.

This potion is carried on fairy wings

and scatters when the wind whistles and sings.

On St. Patrick's Lane, leprechauns abound!

And bright rainbows spring up over the ground.

Each day, the leprechauns make the world's gold,

forging coins for each pot, shiny and bold.

Leprechauns are eager, busy, and green;

they love to play tricks, but are never mean!

Each Tuesday morning they plant four-leafed clover,

tending each bud and leaf over and over.

When rainbows are sprouted, just one is intended,

though extras, a bit smaller, grow up so splendid.

Rainbows are meant to be spun only one time per week.

Yet leprechauns spin them each day for colors they seek.

How leprechauns make rainbows remain a mystery,

and is bound to remain so throughout history.

Just as it is unknown how twelve reindeer can fly,

rainbow secrets are guarded by feisty green guys.

It is rare that rainbows all look the same,

each sparkles and shimmers, not one is plain.

Every known color twinkles within,

with bold vivid stripes and bright sparkling gems.

Sometimes leprechauns forget rainbows are hot.

If they touch one too soon they then jump and trot.

Always shining and strong, rainbows are bright;

in the dark they are a great source of light.

Fluffy bunnies hop and bop up Easter Street,

while gnomes with feather hats make candy Peeps.

They boil and decorate thousands of eggs,

and bunnies spill colors with each bounce of their legs.

Emmitt Brown is the name of the Easter Bunny.

He romps in Gommet's green fields, so bright and sunny.

His house is just outside the garden wall,

where gnomes plant sunflowers many miles tall.

Easter Street has an abundance of daisies,

tulips, and pansies because gnomes are not lazy!

No harsh cold winters keep them from blooming,

and the wind's gentle breeze sends their scents zooming.

Households throughout the world share Easter cheer,

bundling baskets of goodies to happily share.

The bunnies help Emmitt visit houses and stores.

But on this street it's the gnomes who take on most chores.

It's not at all spooky on Halloween Court.

There are no haunted houses of any sort.

Fun houses were haunted before they shut down;

fun houses bring smiles, haunted houses cause frowns.

Long ago, when haunted houses stood here,

ghosts shouted "boo!" and wreaked havoc and fear.

Creaking, squeaking, and groaning were real issues,

then Leprechauns cried and used all the tissues.

Doors were oiled to remove all the creaking.

Mirrors and windows were added for peeking.

Houses were painted bright yellow, no longer black.

Music plays through the doors, both the front and the back.

Leprechauns and gnomes fill the fun houses with giggles,

through crooked doorways and twisty tunnels they wiggle.

Funny faces in bright frames plaster the walls,

while gnomes jump in the pit of round, bouncy balls.

The Court is lined with multi-colored trees

that sprout thick batches of crispy, bright leaves.

Some pumpkins banded together to form a group.

Named the Autumn Tribe, they are a merry troupe.

The group decides how much candy corn to make,

scarecrows to stuff and orange cookies to bake.

They design and sew all the Halloween costumes,

and teach witches to fly over the bright Harvest Moon.

The Autumn Tribe watches movies and shows

to learn about characters all the kids know.

This is how the most current costumes are made,

otherwise, they would be old-fashioned and fade.

Some costumes are timeless and stay forever,

since they come from stories deeply cherished and clever,

with characters like Snow White or Santa Claus,

or spunky Dorothy from The Wizard of Oz.

Halloween food and smells are brewed on the court.

Apple cider, pumpkins, and donuts of all sorts.

Smells of roasting food seep through from the next drive,

to tantalize and keep all the senses alive.

Turkeys strut around farms on Thanksgiving Drive.

Pilgrims peel and core apples then bake them in pies.

The safe place for turkeys is where the path narrows,

since turkeys are scared of Cupid's flying arrows.

A neat thing about the village of Gommet

is that Thanksgiving Drive has lots of orange on it.

Leaves, pumpkins, orange squash mix in varying hues;

on the Drive you'll find Thanksgiving anytime you choose.

Gommet has one restaurant, Gobble Diner.

Where great food is concerned, there is no finer.

The pilgrims are simply amazing cooks,

but their recipes won't be found in any book.

Pilgrim Ellen is in charge of the eatery.

She does a great job, but she sure is jittery.

Dancing and laughing, she is certainly funny,

her character is always zany and sunny.

This special diner is open around the clock.

It's a friendly place where hungry ghosts like to flock.

Scarecrows don't sleep so they work a few hours,

baking and stirring with their great cooking powers.

Squawking turkeys keep Thanksgiving Drive loud,

while the sky above swims with light, gorgeous clouds.

Autumn colors are sprinkled with dustings of snow

until the wind comes along and off the snow blows.

Christmas Boulevard is a merry ole place.

Santa visits showing his bright, rosy face.

Younger elves live here, but older elves do not.

The North Pole needs elder elves in that chilly spot.

Santa's helpers train under his careful direction.

They strive to become old Saint Nick's reflection.

Santa's visits are frequent and oodles of fun.

It's great when he brings Mrs. Claus's homemade buns.

St. Nick and his wife Betty enjoy their courtship,

so he brings her along on all his Gommet trips.

Betty and the elves love to play hide and seek,

with games known to go on for weeks and weeks.

Because Santa visits but does not live here,

his trips are made with the aid of his reindeer.

While elder elves glue, carve, paint, and shine toys up North,

the reindeer grow strong flying the Clauses back and forth.

Young elves construct toys in Gommet – it's their goal –

until they are next transferred to the North Pole.

The gifts they make are for all the Gommet creatures.

The greatest honor is when an elf's work is featured.

Elves shape, paint, and shine Gommet's mailbox digits.

They design and sew pajamas for Santa's visits.

Elves add jingle to bells on Gobble Diner's front door

and create earrings for Mrs. Claus's jewelry drawer.

The hats Leprechauns wear are sewn by young elves,

the bright outfits gnomes wear don't make themselves!

Elves create the beautiful clothing characters wear,

their clothing always fits perfectly and won't snag or tear.

Did you know that elves can sing Christmas carols?

Yep, all the classics, including "Hark the Herald."

Caroling is a nighttime pleasure that all elves love.

Their favorite song is about two turtle doves.

At times, reindeer and elves do not get along,

like when elves can't keep from bursting into song.

Reindeer close their eyes at night; they need sleep for their flights.

But in Gommet, some elves sing morning, noon, and night.

The greatest number of evergreens can be found

up and down the Christmas Boulevard grounds.

Just the right amount of snow sprinkles all around,

to build Frosty's big body, jaunty and sound.

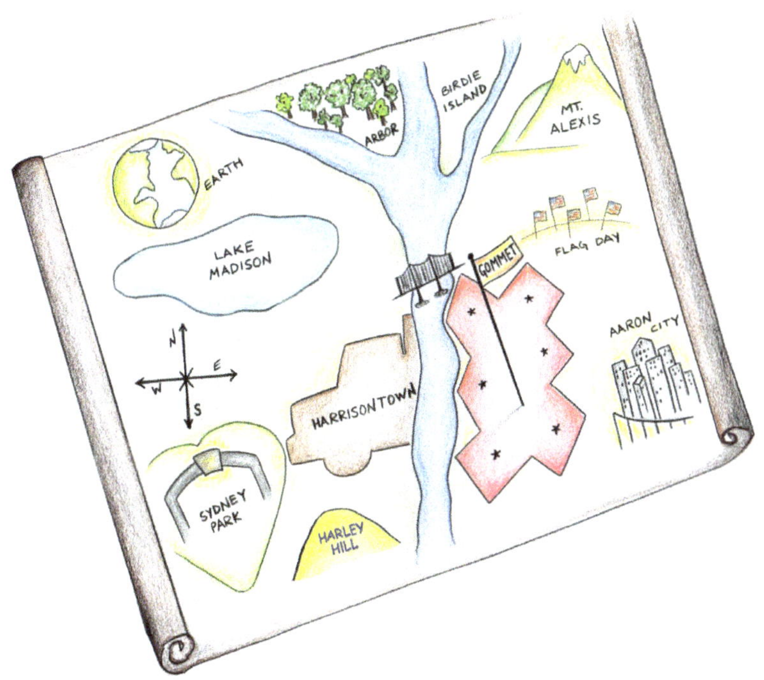

With bright characters and busy working hands,

neighboring villages create holidays on their lands.

Arbor, Earth, and Flag Day are only a few nearby,

each with bright decorations and their own kind of pie.

When you see a rainbow, pumpkin, or Christmas tree,

remember that Gommet made it with love and glee.

Work is never done and characters never age.

Each day is fresh as special plans are laid.

ABOUT THE AUTHOR

Felicity was born and raised in a small New England town in Upstate New York. She could often be found carrying a notebook and pencil, jotting down stories. She loved the arts-reading, writing, acting and singing in school plays and musicals, and playing the piano. She was active in her church, teaching and participating in several youth programs.

Felicity's love for the autumn season began at a young age when the smells of leaves, pumpkins, and apple cider motivated her to jot down ideas for a holiday book. The ideas for this book continued as the years passed and would become her first children's book, Where the Holidays Go.

www.thefelicityfoxhouse.com

COMING SOON

Watch for the other books in the Gommet Series, COMING SOON!

Gommet's Beginnings: Where the Holidays Started

Gommet's Expansions: Where the Holidays Went

Gommet's Confusion: Where the Holidays Mixed-Up

Then, join us for the WHERE THE HOLIDAYS GO events.

See website for all things Gommet!